For Helen and Marceau

The songs of
Sally
Scaredy-pants

Anne Lemonnier   Claire de Gastold

BERBAY
PUBLISHING

Holy moley, the monsters are up bright and early today! The moment Sally opens the apartment door she finds herself face to face with the stairway wolf.

Sally has important things planned for today, but this could be just the start of her troubles. Who knows what lies in wait outside?

To give herself courage, she makes up a little song:

> Horrible wolf,
> with your ugly long snout,
> I can't stop and chat,
> I have to go out.
>
> Away with those claws,
> they cause me no fear.
> So be a good fellow,
> and just disappear!

As if by magic the wolf takes flight, and Sally makes it to the bottom of the stairs. But she's not out of the woods yet: a band of crazy creatures is waiting for her in the hallway.

"Psst, psst, Miss Scaredy-pants," hisses the slithery snake.

"Chopped little girls' livers, that's what I Iike," growls the greedy old bear.

"This way, my pretty!" pipes the preening penguin, performing a pirouette.

Then, in a quaking, quavering voice, sounding oh so polite, Sally sings a new little ditty:

> Honoured beasts,
> please let me through,
> I have some special
> shopping to do.
>
> I ask you please,
> please clear the way.
> I must make it
> to the shops today.
>
> I ask you please,
> be nice, be kind.
> I'll be off right now,
> if you don't mind.

Those guys were really scary! Luckily, Sally makes it through the front door and a breath of warm spring air blows that nightmare away.

But no sooner has she set out than she notices, right in front of her, an enormous eye gleaming in the dark insides of a delivery van. Sally stops dead in her tracks.

Fishy monster,
black and blue,
you make me really
scared of you.

You don't need
sharp teeth to scare,
with your glassy eye
and your unblinking stare.

You're coming at me.
Time to flee!
I'm off and running,
can't catch me!

Sally doesn't slow down until she reaches the coffee roaster's shop. She is out of breath, so the shopkeeper puts down his bag of coffee beans and makes her a hot chocolate. Sally is delighted.

However…

Golden eyes
in a bag of beans,
and long cat's whiskers.
I fear that means…

Now bounding,
springing across the floor,
with a mighty leap
and a mighty roar…

He's on the counter,
a jungle beast.
I fear I'll be
his chosen feast.

But then, in a flash, the leopard scuttles back to his hideout inside the bag of coffee beans. Sally has had a real fright but her songs seem to be working!

She asks the shopkeeper for the first special ingredient she needs: a big block of chocolate. She pops it in her bag and heads off.

Little by little, Sally regains her good spirits. It's not long before she is walking past the greengrocer's stall. Suddenly she senses a mocking gaze. She stands stock still and sings a new song…

> I saw him move,
> I heard him squawk,
> with his wicked beak,
> I heard him talk!
>
> What a pain
> in his feathered suit,
> flapping here
> amongst the fruit!

The other customers stare at Sally, making her feel very embarrassed. She blushes even more deeply when she sees that the poor old parrot perched on the counter is made of papier-mâché. She quickly pays for three pears, straightens her glasses and sets off again.

Sally needs just one more ingredient: cinnamon powder. She will add just a pinch of this "pixie dust" and this will make all the difference.

The spice merchant's stall is at the end of the Gallery of India, opposite the White Elephant restaurant. On the way there she recounts all the magical rhymes of that wacky morning…

Sally is now in the kingdom of a thousand smells, eagerly inspecting all the labels on the spices. But when she glances behind her she is in for a shock: the elephant from the restaurant is waiting for her at the door. Sally tries to breathe calmly and, without taking her eyes off the fearsome beast, she makes up a new rhyme:

Coriander, saffron gold,
Sally brave, Sally bold!

Paprika from old Bombay
I send this creature on its way!

Turmeric and pepper black,
I'll never let this monster back.

Cardamom and cinnamon
elephant, I say 'Begone!'

It worked! The elephant disappeared!
A man in a turban smiles and hands Sally a packet of cinnamon. She continues happily on her way.

On her way home, Sally stops at The Seadog Café. "I've really earned this!" she thinks, as she sips her drink. Suddenly she notices a weird assortment of fish in the café window. Sally makes a face: "Oh no, not again!"

Halibut, hake
are you real or fake?

Whiting frightening?
Give me a break!

For swordfish and ray,
I've a new spell today!

Whale sharks and gropers
I zap you away!

Sally arrives home at last. The whole place is silent, yet she senses that she is not entirely alone. Maybe the stairway wolf is still after her.

When she reaches the top of the stairs she turns around suddenly and – surprise, surprise! – they are *all* there! Sally bursts out laughing, for she is no longer afraid.

It's time to get baking for a special new arrival!

Sally hears her parents' footsteps outside the apartment door. They are back from the maternity hospital. The house smells of chocolate and Sally's mummy is so happy to see her again. Mummy introduces Martin, Sally's brand-new little brother. He looks so fragile, so unsure of himself. Sally takes him gently in her arms and, in front of her astonished parents, sings this strange lullaby:

Horrible wolf,
with your ugly long snout,
you don't belong here,
I'm sending you out.

Sleep, little brother,
the wolf's gone away,
I'm here to protect you
all night and all day.

First English edition published in 2014 by Berbay Publishing Pty Ltd
English translation © Berbay Publishing Pty Ltd 2014
www.berbaybooks.com
PO Box 133, Kew East, 3102, Victoria, Australia
First published by © L'Atelier du Poisson Soluble, 2010
Les chansons de Lalie Frisson, written by Anne Lemonnier
and illustrated by Claire de Gastold

English adaptation by Michael Sedunary
Typesetting: Kylie Hall
National Library of Australia
Cataloguing-in publication data:
Lemonnier, Anne
The Songs of Sally Scaredy-pants

For primary school children
ISBN 978-0-9806711-6-2